AR PTS: 0.5

THE STORY OF WOLVERINE

Adapted by Thomas Macri

Illustrated by Val Semeiks and Hi-Fi Design

Based on the Marvel comic book series Wolverine

ABDO
Spotlight

MARVEL

New York

WWW.ABDOPUBLISHING.COM

Reinforced library bound edition published in 2015 by Spotlight, a division of ABDO
PO Box 398166, Minneapolis, Minnesota 55439. Spotlight produces high-quality
reinforced library bound editions for schools and libraries. Published by Marvel Press,
an imprint of Disney Book Group.

Printed in the United States of America, North Mankato, Minnesota.
052014
072014

marvelkids.com
© MARVEL

THIS BOOK CONTAINS
RECYCLED MATERIALS

CATALOGING-IN-PUBLICATION DATA

Macri, Thomas.
The story of Wolverine / adapted by Thomas Macri ; illustrated by Val Semeiks and
Hi-Fi Design.
p. cm. -- (World of reading. Level 2)
Summary: Learn how James Howlett became the super hero known as Wolverine.
1. Wolverine (Fictitious character)--Juvenile fiction. 2. Mutation (Biology)--Juvenile
fiction. 3. Superheroes--Juvenile fiction. I. Val Semeiks, ill. II. Hi-Fi Colour Design, ill.
III. Title. IV. Series.
[E]--dc23

978-1-61479-262-8 (Reinforced Library Bound Edition)

Spotlight
A Division of ABDO
www.abdopublishing.com

James grew up in a big house.
It was in the mountains. He played
with his friends, Rose and Dog.

The kids grew up together.

When they were young they'd play tag.

As they got older they hiked and fished.

Dog and his father were poor.
James and his father were rich.
Dog and his father were jealous
and angry.

One night, the father and son
kicked in James's door.
They broke into his house.

Dog's father wanted to hurt James's father. James was frightened!

James's hands started to feel
strange. He looked at them. He
didn't know what was happening.

His hands started to shake.

Claws popped out of his hands!
He didn't know what to do.

James was in pain.
The claws hurt!

James's claws went back into his
hands. The scars healed right away!
He could not be hurt! People would
think he was a freak. Rose had a plan
to save him.

She grabbed his hand and they ran
as fast as they could.

They sneaked onto a train. They were going to run far from home. They'd go somewhere no one would know them.

They arrived in a snowy place. They met a man name Smitty. He was a miner.

James went to work for him.
He pushed carts full of coal.
He changed his name to Logan.
This would help him lay low.

Logan grew older. He never stopped working hard.

He used an ax to chop lumber.

He hunted with a spear.

But most of all he loved being in
the wild. There he could use
his claws. It was the only place he
could truly be himself.

One day while Logan was having
dinner, two men came and
kidnapped him.

They hooked him up to machines.
The machines gave him metal claws!

Logan escaped from the lab.
He ran out into the snow.
It was so cold ice formed on his
metal claws.

He was saved by two Super Heroes.
They were called Vindicator
and Guardian.
They gave him a costume.
They gave him a Super Hero name.

They called him the Wolverine!

He became part of a team.
They were called Alpha Flight.

He also fought alone.
One of the first times he did this,
he fought the Hulk.

The two heroes locked in battle.
It was a very even fight.
Neither of them won.

Wolverine met the X-Men.

Professor X was their leader.

He told Wolverine that he was
a mutant.

The X-Men were mutants, too.

They were born with their powers.

Logan had always felt alone.

But now he knew others like him.

The X-Men were outsiders, too.

And with the X-Men, Wolverine had found a family.